When I've recovered from this, I'm punting you into the
sun where you belong. Burning to dust among the
cosmos.

–King, Jester

WILDFORGED

WILDFORGED

A.C. BAUER

MEMENTO VIVERE PRESS

Published by MEMENTO VIVERE PRESS
www.mementoviverepress.com
First Edition, May 2025

Publisher, Ynes Freeman
ynes@mementoviverepress.com

Formatter, Leo Otherland
leo@mementoviverepress.com

Cover art by Rue Sparks
www.ruesparks.com

Cover design by Sianyn Leigh
www.chaosinkbooks.com/staff-bio

Print ISBN: 978-1-964501-06-2
Ebook ISBN: 978-1-964501-07-9

Once upon a not-so-distant time, across the not-so-distant peaks of the Spine that split Avetri, there lived a woman. Her hair was harnessed midnight; her eyes were poured from the cold, fathomless blue of the Norsea; her hands—blackened, twisted, and scarred, were little more than talons. She was of the wild, and the wild lived in her. The power of raw chaos—of destruction and undoing, the end of all things—blanketed her very bones, and even her fellow mages could not comprehend the breadth of that power.

And yet, sunshine lived in her smile. Kindness danced along her corrupted skin. Her tongue, with its knife-sharp wit and deadly precision, was always lifted in song. Because the nature of the wild is this: there is beauty in transformation, in endings, and in breaking down. So despite others' distrust, she wielded her power with pride and was unafraid of it.

She was but a woman, frail and mortal, but the world did not see her as such. They mantled her with godhood, cast her as a monstrosity. For a long time, that was all right. She had never been a stranger to unkindness, but knew she could not make them understand. All she asked was to wander, keeping doom at her heels, and to aid the world in its labors.

But she did not hold herself to the same standards as the common mages. When chaos spoke, she listened, and those left behind when her work was done—the children, the siblings, the husbands and wives and friends and never-quite-lovers—came to revile her. Their mourning keens morphed into a united cry of anger, to a cry of "monster," to a cry of a hound stumbling upon an elusive trail. They did not understand the gifts she shared: not death's kindness or cleansing fire or bitter storms that washed away the rotten foundations of old lives.

They chased her across the mountains to a city that was not a city, but a ramshackle hamlet where sellswords congregated. Baneston was, at first, kind. Understanding. But the one thing a mercenary needs, above all else, is coin. And when the ruling House Erus, with their unlimited pockets, began to offer coin for mages' whereabouts, she learned that some she considered to be friends were not friends at all.

So she fled, with chaos in her bones and a child seeded in her belly, back across the Spine and into the heart of the north, making her home in the forest far from any who might seek to harm her.

At the same time, far below the Spine and nestled in the southern lap of luxury, there lived a man. He, too, carried magic in him, but he did not suffer it gracefully. He did not smile, nor did he sing, nor did he offer himself as a catalyst for change. He feared. He cowered. He carved out tales of the god in the north—who was not much of a god at all—from mages captured by the crown. And he was at first revered by those who held his leash, because in the same way there is beauty in destruction, there is danger in creation. *Resurrection* became synonymous with his torture, and the world came to fear his name.

Save for that used in his work, the mage hoarded his power, and at first, the capital city of Aethrun flourished around him. But magic—either side of the coin, chaos or creation—craves a purpose. It craves guidance as much as it craves freedom, but if it is not given one, it will take the other. As the mage's magic bled into the world without his intention to guide it, massive hardwoods began to choke the eastern castle walls. To the west, farms struggled under the increased duty demanded by overfull fields and unmanageable herds. Inside Aethrun's walls, people could barely move through the streets.

Everything became untameable.

The man—who was himself not a god, but as frail and mortal as the woman chaos chose—continued to deny his place in all of it until House Erus declared the Culling. The south fork of the Aethrun River ran red with the blood of people and animals alike, and the man was sickened. Repulsed by the magic in him, in every other mage, and in the world itself.

When the queen sent him northward, an extension of the crown's hand meant to choke out all magic, he went without complaint. His inquisition, too, left mourners in its wake, and the people of Avetri—mages and non-mages alike—began to regret turning the woman away, because she and she alone held enough magic to repel this southern threat.

At the end of all things, across the Spine and under freezing winter skies, the man and the woman found one another. She approached him with kindness; he showed her a blade. Their battle was a fierce, vicious thing, merciless and wild. Like two glowing pieces of iron struck together against an anvil, the magic shed by their battle was sculpted into something new: a roiling mass of power that grew unchecked even as it cannibalized itself.

When the battle was finished, two ruined bodies lay below the freezing sky, surrounded by a splintered forest. As the earth leached their blood, so, too, did it leach this new magic. But there was no one left to watch their bones seed the world with ruin. No one to stop it. No one to care.

No one save a child, freshly torn from its mother's belly, that did not—*could* not—die.

ΦΦΦ

The sky is pissing rain for the fourth night in a row when Felix Grey feels the presence of the mage he's been tracking drawing nearer to the Black Hen. He leans back against one of the inn's wooden support beams and sweeps his gaze across the common room, eyes narrowed in concentration. The crowd is sparse tonight—no new faces, only the usual folk deep in their cups. A few of them *could* be mages—he feels the gentle fluttering of magic trapped in them like a butterfly's wings against his cheek—but none have quickened. Moreover, this presence speaks of power far beyond any mage he's encountered.

It settles around him and tastes like summer: heat, and fresh-cut hay, and just-plucked peach, and the first sip of creek water after a long day on the road. The magic itself claws at him, as though seeking entrance to his body, and he shudders as his own chaos repels the foreign energy.

It's strange for any mage worth their salt to be in Aethrun to begin with.

It's downright suicidal to bleed magic so freely.

"You're not luring anyone to bed with that scowl, lad." Felix spooks as Reiva—the Black Hen's mistress—claps a hand on his shoulder. "Easy, love," she continues. Her brow is furrowed as she leans close. "There's a girl at the back gate. Just a little mite, looks liable to drown out in this weather." She tucks her lip between her teeth. "I'm not buying it."

"She's the one?"

Reiva nods. Felix trusts her judgement: of all his contacts, she has proven the most reliable when it comes to tracking down his marks. "Throw a loaf of that cheese bread you like so much in your pack tomorrow if you take care of it quietly."

"Look at you, being so generous."

"Tsk." Reiva swats his arm with the back of her hand, but chuckles. "Can't afford to have the Queensguard sniffing around."

Felix grunts his assent and shoves off the post, weaving his way back through the inn's common room toward the single door leading into the small yard behind the attached stable. He slips one of his smaller knives into his palm and tucks the blade up against his wrist, takes a steadying breath, and eases the door open.

Lightning splits the sky and illuminates the woman, whose eyes flash when she catches sight of Felix. He takes several steps back on instinct. So close and with nothing between them but empty air, her magic batters him from all sides, howling and doing its best to knock him to his knees.

He has never known power like this.

"*You,*" the mage says.

Felix's mouth twists sourly as he tightens his grip on his knife. "Control yourself," he says, low and dangerous, "or you will bring the whole of House Erus down on *both* our heads."

The woman's long blonde hair whips against her face as wind blows the sheeting rain into them. She hoists her palms to her shoulders in a gesture of nonviolence, but she does nothing to rein her presence in. Already, Felix sees the browned winter grass beginning to green around her. "You're her, aren't you?"

"Poor form to fling your magic all over the city and then call your savior a woman." Felix's stomach knots as he steps forward once, twice, and leans closer to peer into her eyes. He thinks, fleetingly, she does not look afraid enough to be facing down an equally powerful mage.

Thinking is his first mistake.

The woman darts forward, quicker than Felix expects, and his back hits the wall before he kicks her shin, throws her to the ground, and kneels on both arms as he digs the point of his dagger into her chin.

"Who the fuck do you think you are?" he hisses.

"Where have you been hiding?"

"Answer me."

The woman purses her lips. Around them, thunder rolls. He's moments away from making a quick end of her when she says, "I don't know how to stop it. I—They never taught . . ."

Felix does not soften his hold, but says, "You need to hold it. Breathe. *Breathe . . .* Good." Her pulse thrums below the palm he presses to her neck, and her breath is thin with panic, but she tries. "Picture that power. Cage it. Force it into submission. Can you do that for me?"

Breath by trembling breath, she does. The wild edges of her magic are tucked away one by one until her presence feels more like late summer warmth rather than the sun itself. It's not good enough, but it will have to do.

"Now," he says, quiet but no less deadly. "Your name."

"Moira."

"When did your magic quicken, Moira?"

"Years ago."

Felix's face screws in disgust, but no small amount of pity courses through him. "And no one has taught you even the most *basic* of courtesies? And everyone hides in Aethrun, except you. Do you *want* to be thrown in a dungeon?"

"No! I-I'm sorry." Her voice is smaller now, shaky. Her eyes flick from side to side and she allows him to press her further into the dirt as she says, "I just felt you. I *feel* you, and you're . . . like me, I think."

"There are plenty of mages scattered across Avetri."

"Not like us. Not powerful." She swallows hard.

"You're afraid," he says, brooking no argument. "Are you running from something, Moira?"

Moira blanches. "Yes. Er, sort of. Yes."

Felix is no stranger to flight. He is no stranger to the myriad happenings that might force someone into the sheeting rain without the knowledge or even *instincts* to survive a new environment. (Because this is new to Moira—that fact is written across every part of her, from her pale skin to the fine cut of her clothing to the lack of manners.) He is also no stranger to liars.

Cagey and brash as she might be, Moira is not lying. The fear in her eyes is genuine.

He makes a decision.

"I think we've gotten off on several wrong feet." Felix makes a show of sheathing his knife and rocking back onto his heels, freeing Moira's arms. He heaves himself to his feet and holds his hand out to her. "Come. Convince me you're worth the risk I'm taking by letting you live."

◊◊◊

The child that could not die grew into a child that did not quite understand how to live. It spent its first few years amidst the wolves, under the watchful eye of the she-wolf that found it squalling and starving in the midst of the sundered earth. The pack was its family as much as the wind in the trees and the rain that soaked the field, and it loved them dearly.

The child had traveled five summers with the wolves when the world around it began to reek of corruption. The normal forest scent was chased away by that of fruit rotting on the vine; the familiar animals with bizarre creatures too frightening to hunt; and the trees with twisted, choked husks that never seemed quite alive. And when the pack and its prey could no longer live in harmony with this new world, the not-wolf joined them on the journey south.

It spent many long months on the run as the pack carved out its new territory, doing its best to keep up with their easy loping gaits as they forged forward. But despite its efforts, it was not a wolf. It was slow, and sickly, and stupid, and so it buried itself in the last of the winter snows to wait out its end.

It waited.

It grew fragile.

It waited.

Hunger hollowed out its belly.

It waited.

Death did not come.

Something inside of it writhed and roiled, sustaining it even despite its aching need for a peaceful demise. It felt its body wax and wane like the moon above: when it grew too weak, the strange power fortified it; before it could grow too strong, an opposing force began to gnaw at that newfound glory.

The first chill winds of autumn had begun to blow when it crawled out of its den and stumbled across the flat, empty stretch of mud that's always better left avoided. Behind it, the rotten stink of a beast caught in the Sundering grew ever-stronger. Ahead, it heard the dull thud of hooves and a raucous braying noise that gated on its sensitive ears.

It was alone, and it was weak. No pack, no protection.

It chose.

It sprinted forward, breathing hard as it skidded to a stop in front of the herd of horses bearing strange, partially-furred creatures on their backs. Its howl silenced their braying, but did nothing to alert them to the encroaching danger.

When it came upon them, the thing that was once a bear, the child shrank away from the roar of battle. Its claws were brittle and its teeth dull; over and over again, it had learned to remain out of sight. It had learned to watch its packmates fall, and these new creatures fell in the same way, bloody and stinking of recent death.

But when it was over, many of the creatures— which looked far more like it than its wolven brethren— stood on their hind legs and screamed their anger to the cloudy sky. The child shoved itself farther below the cover of a fir tree and yelped with fury when strong paws caught its ankles and pulled it into the open. It did not understand their barking, nor did it trust the light glinting off the long claws they kept clutched tight. It bit and scratched and yowled, but even so, its saviors turned to captors, and all it could do was watch from a horse's back as its home drew farther and farther away.

Across all of Avetri, there is one simple rule regarding the discussion, study, and wielding of magic: do not, under any circumstances.

Felix, along with every other Avetran mage, has never been good at following the rules. He has never been opposed to activities—if he's painting theft and treason and murder in the kindest light—that fall outside the realm of legality. One does not grow up in the City of Swords and retain their innocence. Still, he cannot help but be shocked at the flippant way Moira brushes aside even the simplest safeguards every mage learns upon their quickening, not the least of which is carrying a book filled with what she claims is her collected research on the Sundering.

"It's all here," she says, scoffing and shoving the leather-bound tome across the small table in his room. "Krynn, Kestra, his hunt, the crown's quest to—er—" She breaks off and chews on the sentence for a bit before deciding on, "Manage the effects of magic."

"Killing mages, you mean."

At least she has the decency to avert her eyes when she agrees.

Felix leans back in his chair and stretches his arms above his head with a low groan. His instincts have proven correct: after a meal and several stern glances from Reiva, Moira meekly let slip that she's been sequestered behind castle walls her whole life. Over the course of the night, he's ferreted out bits and pieces of the story, but not enough to form the whole picture. Despite this, he knows several things.

One: Moira is, despite her initial burst of bravado, not a fighter. She puffs herself up and yowls when Felix prods her toward answers she doesn't want to give, but that veneer shatters when she latches onto something she's eager to share, because Moira is a *scholar.*

Two: Moira is not unkind. Brash, yes. Easy to rile, yes. Unkind only when she fumbles her way into topics she does not understand, or that are better left undisturbed.

Three, relatedly: Not only is Moira not versed in the mores of magehood—she isn't versed in the ways of the world outside court at all. If the thought of doing so didn't make him sick to his stomach, Felix might take her for all she's worth and leave her to rot below a tree somewhere. She would make it easy.

And thus, most importantly, four: Moira needs protection.

He holds his hand out. "Give me the book."

"You won't throw it in the fire."

It's an order, not a question—and, he has to admit, not unwarranted after his reaction to finding such a book existed in the first place—but Felix answers, "Unlike some people, I can accept an offer with grace. I solemnly swear not to torch your little journal."

And he doesn't. Instead, he sits in the mid-afternoon quiet and flips idly through the book, basking in the silence as his veins fill with ice. The first bit is old news: two mages, each a hero in their own eyes. Their flight. Their fight. The resulting wound that sundered the land. Felix has heard the story of Kestra and Krynn many, many times over the years.

It is the next several dozen pages that give him pause. Row after row of names are scrawled across the paper—some with a series of notes scribbled next to them, some crossed out with a single brutal slash mark, some with no markings at all.

He *recognizes* many of these people.

Felix snaps the book shut and looks up. "Why keep track of mages like this? *How?* Keeping this inside the *castle,* Moira, have you lost your damned mind?"

Moira leans forward to rest both elbows on the table and pinches the bridge of her nose, sighing out a breath that ends in a frustrated growl. "Can you leave the scolding and just—" She holds her hands in front of her, cupped but about a foot apart, and glares at him. "Listen. What do you see when you look at me?"

"A pain in my ass, if I'm honest."

She narrows her eyes further.

Felix grunts, but doesn't take it back before tossing her a bone. "Your power."

"*Exactly.* Most mages aren't like that. Like us." She brings her hands together, just a brief space between them now. "They're like candles. Brief flashes of power, there and gone. Some—the particularly talented—I'd call a torch. I've even come across a few...oh, we'll call them hearth fires. But you?" She claps her hands before throwing her arms wide. "You're a forest fire, Felix, even with the hold you've got on yourself. I could feel you all the way inside the keep.

"Queen Audra—no, don't give me that look; I need you to hear this—is not unreasonable. She is not her mother, who forced my father's hand, and she is not a fool. Despite the court's prevailing prejudice toward mages, she was willing to listen to me when I approached her with my findings.

"I believe the Sundering can be fixed, Felix. I've scoured every scroll and book in the keep, and spoken with my aunt's informan—"

"Your what." Felix's voice is as flat as the tabletop.

"My aunt. Keep up. I've spoken with her infor—"

"Your father. Krynn. Your aunt is the fucking *queen*?"

Moira blinks. "Yes?"

Felix buries his face in both hands and screams through gritted teeth before breathing deep and wheezing, "Continue."

"She's not so bad," Moira mumbles.

"The crown's killed friends. Family. You'll forgive the skepticism. Did she just *let* you go? Are they searching for you?"

"Listen!" The table leaps when Moira's hand slaps down hard. If Felix wasn't frozen to his chair, he might have jumped. Instead, he just gapes as she says, "If we can reverse the damage, she thinks there's a real chance to pave a new way forward. Make people revere magecraft again, rather than fear it."

She picks up the book and flips through it until she makes a soft exclamation and spreads the page—notes about flora and fauna harvested from the affected land—in front of him, stabbing at it with a finger.

"I've seen these. *Studied* them, and the magical energy they carry. The rotting stuff. And I think that, with sufficient power—" she gestures between them, then circles her hand to point in every direction "—with enough mages working together, we might be able to draw the rot out and separate those magics. The mages. And you. And me. Guiding."

When Felix stops laughing long enough to hear Moira out, he is dismayed beyond measure to realize that she's speaking *sense.* Worse, she plans to ride to Baneston and then across the Spine with or without him. (He has no doubt that without him, she will, at best, reach the Aethrun gates.) And, to force his hand, she tells this over dinner to Reiva, who smiles sweetly and says, "Isn't it about time for you to be heading up that way for the summer?"

"See if I ever do a job for you again," he complains at her later that night, when Moira is sleeping and it's just him and Reiva drinking behind the bar. "That was cruel."

"Oh, please," Reiva says, waving a dismissive hand. "Like you would've said no."

"I might've!"

But he doesn't, and they ride out after several days of planning. Felix side-eyes Moira's new mare as they walk side by side, wary after she nearly took a chunk out of his arm earlier that morning. Moira seems content to ignore this fact and coos at the beast—Daisy—until Aethrun is behind them and Felix urges his own mount—Dirk, the black gelding he's had for over a decade—into a canter.

The rolling hills of the southern peninsula fly by as they soak in the sun that's decided to show itself after weeks. It is good to be in the saddle again; Aethrun, though kind to his purse, does not scratch the itch that draws him to wander. It's a nice enough place to winter for a month or two before picking his way north up the coast. (Any local will tell you it gets bitter cold in Aethrun; any foreigner will laugh and call it mild at best. Felix is confident that Baneston's kindest summer days are cooler than the bitterest Avetran winter day.)

The first week is a quiet thing. It rains on and off, and they do their best to find shelter where they can. On nights when they cannot rest their heads in a stable or outbuilding, Felix posts himself on watch. This far south, the chances of running across dreaders are slim, but not nonexistent, and Felix has the distinct impression that Moira would not live to sound the alarm.

Felix wishes he were a stranger to the beasts' corrupted nature. Every time he thinks he's seen it all, more—and in worse shape than before—bleeds over the Spine to wreak havoc on vulnerable villages. The beasts are the embodiment of the Sundering's bastardized magic: not alive, never dead, and always starving. It is not their fault. An animal is a product of its environment, and when the very land it lives off of is rotting, that rot spreads.

That does not make them any more pleasant to deal with.

They bed down in an inn just outside of Eastford for their first night. Felix elects to take care of the horses and allow Moira to do the haggling, and that proves to be the correct choice when he walks into the sight of warm food and a bath. The homey scent of roasted meat and spices is underscored by the crusty bread on a plate next to it. Winter vegetables are piled high in a bowl, glazed and steaming. The water in the basin even looks warm.

He whistles. "Impressive. Tired of stinking like the road?"

Moira flicks her fingers at him irritatedly and scrunches her nose as she chews her fresh mouthful of food. "You first."

Felix glances around the room for a screen or curtain. When he comes up empty, he says, "You're not planning on *watching*."

"I can turn around."

The swift dismissal rankles him.

Felix's body is a battleground. Scars of every kind—from lacy knife work courtesy of a particularly exacting fuck to patchy burns from mishaps in his father's forge—are his own twisted diary, a map of the places he's been and people he's hurt. He's put some there himself. But where Moira is more than content to spill her secrets to anyone she deems necessary to further her agenda, Felix is cautious. More reticent. He's long since grown tired of the way people look at him with revulsion, or worse, pity.

When she notices his hesitation, she softens. "I'll make myself scarce. *After* I'm done eating."

"Thank you," Felix murmurs. He spears a chunk of meat and tears at it without bothering to hide his hunger. Even now, after nearly three decades of civilization, his body has not overwritten the instinct to gorge when provided with an easy meal after a long day.

"Don't choke," Moira deadpans.

"Fuck you."

The next day dawns watery and gray, but there's warmth in Felix's core, lodged somewhere below his lungs. When Moira breaks out into a loud and very off-key rendition of a popular traveling song as they leave the town behind, he joins her, laughing when Daisy throws her head back to voice her own loud complaints about the noise.

They pass the first signs of trouble several hours later as they're approaching the trade city of Crayden. Blood stains the road, and not a single person is out and about. The city noise itself is muted, as though the very earth is holding its breath.

Felix nudges Dirk forward until he's on top of a thick puddle, and then slides off to take a closer look at the tracks muddying the scene. The human footprints are obvious, all leading toward the tightly sealed city gate. Long claws—longer than reasonable for any normal animal—have gouged into the earth, making it easy to miss the fact the prints just behind the marks have come from twisted paws.

"Dreaders," he says.

"The gates are still barred," Moira says. Her voice is thick as she holds her cloak over her nose, likely doing little to stifle the stench. "Certainly they'd let travelers in, wouldn't they?"

"Keep your voice down," Felix hisses. "There might be more about."

Daisy sidesteps, ears flicking back and forth as she snorts, and Moira shushes her when something clatters near the watchtowers. She squints, then brightens and raises her hand in a wild wave. "Felix, someone's in th—"

She's cut off by the dull thud of an arrow striking the dirt just ahead of her. Daisy startles, nearly backing over Felix and into Dirk, and whinnies.

"Shit. *Shit.*" Moira holds one hand up in surrender while the other scrabbles to hold Daisy's reins. "We mean no harm!" she calls. "We just wanted to—"

The archer does not wait to answer, and the message comes in the form of another arrow landing too close to Felix's feet for comfort. Felix scrambles onto Dirk and they set off at a brisk gallop. When Moira makes to wheel and shout at the assailant, Felix wastes no time in bullying Daisy back into line. "Leave it," he barks, pulling hard on one rein. "We'll find another town."

"But they might need help!"

"From who, you? Yeah, I'm sure they'll fling the doors wide open to a pair of mages on the heels of a magical attack. Come on, Moira, *think*."

"We're people, not beasts," she protests.

"Welcome to the real world." Felix rounds on Daisy to look Moira in the eye, holding her gaze for several long seconds. "This is not your cloistered palace. People do not know who you are. I *guarantee* they have at least one mage in that tower on lookout for more potential threats, and if it were me, I wouldn't take kindly to two strangers blazing with power. Look at me!" He only half regrets how loud it comes out. "If you want to save the thrice-damned north, you have got to understand these things."

"So teach me," she says, just as riled. "Maybe that's how you protect me—you pick up the reins and *help*."

ΦΦΦ

They took the child across the mountains and kept it in a cage just beyond the pass. The other cages—they could not make it understand *house* or *hearth* or even *comfort*—huddled like swallows on a branch, each a dark lump next to its neighbor. And try as they might to tame the child, it refused. It howled and screamed and cried until one day, its noise found a shape.

Its little paws dragged a shining longclaw across the dirt to where its master made his own noise in the forge. It lifted its prize; it dropped its prize. But when its master, who growled like no predator it had ever come across, made to take it from the child, it shook its head and said *No*.

Then, it ran.

Oh, how the chase thrilled it. Even with the new weight of its prize dragging it down, and the crowing of the grayhairs along the way, and the chill of spring nipping at its heels, it bounded down the road on eager legs. The watery sunlight bathed everything in gray, and it felt halfway back to the mountains before thick, gnarled hands wrapped around its shoulders and lifted it, squealing, into the air.

Its master was angry, and then, almost before it knew to cower, its master grew sad. Master pulled it close and rumbled things the child did not yet understand—things that, for the very first time, it found itself *wanting* to understand. Because even now, even after running away, its master's hands were gentle as they put the longclaw back into the child's grip. Master's hands were warm. Master's hands were *kind*.

The longclaw glinted in the light as they swung it together, slow and steady in front of the rest of the gathering pack. All at once, the child found itself exhausted by the weight of things: its struggles, its fears, its unquenchable rage. It sniffled, and then—choking on its own grief—it cried.

Master picked it up and held it close, and it could not find it in itself to struggle. The roughness of his not-fur scratched at the child's cheeks, but soon enough the roughness was traded for its soft nest in the back rooms of the forge, where the master pet it and fed it and did not urge it to speak again. Despite its lingering tears, the child felt a tiny curl of warmth in its chest.

And so, when they both woke late the next morning, it gave its master a name of his own—one it had heard other pups scream at their sires: Da.

Its life was not without hardship in the following seasons. Progress was slow, often one or two steps back per every three forward, but eventually the child grew to understand its place in the town. It suffered the scratchy clothes and chores and the things it was taught because when it tried its best, its da was proud. Happy.

But not even its da could convince it that some things were more proper for a bitch cub than its brothers. It tore at the suffocating layers of cloth its da laid out for it in the mornings and screamed when it was told it needed to be a proper lady. Its world no longer made sense. Gone were the days of helping da at his forge. Gone were the days of frolicking in the streets with its new packmates. Gone were the roughhousing and the hunting and the howling.

And so the bitch cub—who was not a bitch cub, but a snarling knot of regret and disappointment—did the only thing it could.

It fought.

The constant hunger gnawing at its insides seared through it until it was that hunger, and that hunger was *all* it was. Its skin turned black as chaos screamed through it. Its entire body burned with the forces driving it to rip and tear and rend.

And then, it came back to itself in a bed that was not its own with a sickness it had never known. Its skin was pale again. It hurt. It smelled blood, but it could not find the source wound between its legs. When it begged for its da, it was told in no uncertain terms it had to stay put, that da was also injured.

The healer that nursed it back to health was stern, but kind. She told it that it was a marvel, something to be revered and respected, but it did not understand what she meant until she took it into the street and showed it the damage it had wrought. She said, *You have the wild in you.* She said, *It will kill you if you let it.* She said, *Let me show you the mage's way.* Still, she did not let it see its da.

The healer called herself Ysa. The healer did not call the child anything but *you* and *child* and *apprentice* until one day she sat it down and asked it what it wanted to call itself. The child did not know; it had never considered itself to be anything but what others named it. It was then, and only then, that the healer brought it to its da. The forge sat cold, and the steady stream of customers was nowhere to be found as Ysa took the child into the back room.

Immediately it recoiled, because its da was no longer the man it knew. The man on the cot wore its da's smile, but did not look like the man it had grown to love. His left arm—what was left of it—was a withered stump that bled darkness into his torso. His face was also scarred by the darkness the child now recognized as its own magic, and when he attempted to swing himself out of bed, the child wept bitterly when it realized it had taken almost all of his left leg as well.

And yet, its da held his arm out and embraced the child. He said, *I am sorry.* He said, *Forgive me for not believing you.* He said, *I will always love all of you.*

He said, with a tremulous smile, *My son,* and the child cried harder as his da set him on the path to manhood.

In the winter of his sixteenth year, that manhood was bestowed upon the boy.

This did not mean he *felt* like a man.

The man—who was now Felix, who had not been the bitch cub in over two years—approached his father with questions that the smith did not know how to answer. Because Tobin knew Felix, knew his son and knew the child he had been before he was Felix and knew of the wild thing he had been before he was Tobin's child. But Tobin did not know everything, and he did not know how to soothe the ragged edges of the wound that Felix called *mother*.

And so Felix went to Ysa. He asked, *Who was she?* He asked, *Why didn't she want me?* He asked, *Was it my fault?*

But Ysa did not know either, and so Felix remained haunted by the things he did not understand.

Later, quieter, afraid of the answer, he began, *Could she have been . . .*

He did not have the courage to finish the question. He tried to convince himself it did not matter.

When his friends began to have children of their own, he struggled to comprehend the love he saw in their eyes. He did not recognize it. He did not possess it. And despite themselves, they could not help but ask when he would marry and bear a child, because they did not understand his refusal of their greatest joy.

Felix threw himself into his work. At seventeen, he left Baneston with the clothes on his back and the knives he'd forged for himself. At nineteen, he came back hardened. Confident, sure. The road had whittled away the last of his childhood, and he was grateful for it. There was blood on his hands and coin in his purse and a request he spoke plainly to Ysa: *I want to be changed.*

And so Ysa laid him on a table. She said, *This will hurt.* She said, *I'm proud of you.* She said, *Hold my hand—I am here.*

And so Felix was changed. There was no more womb to worry over, no breasts to be bound. There were new scars. There were mournful silences from people he thought might care. More than all of that, there was relief. He was himself: born of the wild, molded by its power, and wielder of its glory.

How could learning the truth about his history make him any more complete?

ΦΦΦ

"Healing? With that?" Moira cants her head to the chaos swirling indolently in Felix's palm. "I don't believe that for a second."

With a flourish, Felix stops drawing on the power and stuffs the hand in his pocket, sticking his tongue between his lips as he struggles to find the coin he shoved in there earlier. They've stopped to water the horses and stretch their aching muscles, and Felix is wont to say they'll camp along the river's edge for the night. They've made good time over the past several days—it wouldn't be so bad to take their time for part of this last leg.

When he locates the copper, he pulls it free with a grin. "Look. If you think of it like this—magic is the coin, yes?" He holds the queen's stamp to her face. "Audra gives to her subjects. She creates. You might heal by making more of something: blood, organs, that sort of thing." He flips the copper to show Moira the treasury stamp.

"Think of chaos as a tax. In order for your body to operate well, it can be helpful to remove that which does not work." He holds one hand to his chest and the other to his lower belly. "It wasn't creation that shaped me, but I became something new." The copper flashes in the sun as he twirls it between his knuckles. "It can be dangerous, though. Humans are complex creatures, which provides plenty of options for choosing how to heal. Or destroy, if that's your choice. I've seen some disgusting applications of power.

"Conversely—" again, he flashes the coin "—it's very easy to kill someone if you're not careful with enhancements."

Moira leans back on her hands and tips her face to the sun, sighing contentedly as she soaks in its warmth. "I suppose you have experience with that, too?"

Felix makes a noncommittal noise and wiggles his hand from side to side. "Not personally, but da's told me about a friend who ended up in the ground because—" He brings a fist to his mouth, which does nothing to stifle his snicker. "Well, apparently he couldn't satisfy his wife."

It takes a minute for her to come around to the point, but when she does, she gasps *"Felix"* and shoves his shoulder, sending him sprawling in the grass. "You prick," she giggles. "He didn't."

"He did! Jumped in the sack and dropped dead, I swear. Or, that's how da tells it." Felix slots both arms behind his head and turns to glance at the horses as his smile fades. "Heart problem," he says. "Tough to know how you're going to affect someone, which makes it *absolutely* necessary to get proper training if you want to heal more than day-to-day injuries. Anyone who hasn't quickened is fair game, but never—" he props himself up and points at himself "—even if you are trained, attempt to use your magic on one of chaos's mages. The magics' reaction will cause your patient far more harm than their wounds."

Moira cocks her head, eyes narrowing as she ponders. "But when I touched you in Aethrun, I felt . . . I thought . . ."

"That hurt, make no mistake."

"Mm."

Felix does not like the contemplative gaze, or the questions he can sense brewing. He does not want to talk about it. "Are you stretched?"

"What? I—Yes." Moira shakes herself out of her reverie and stands, brushing grass off of her trousers and glancing at Felix out of the corner of her eye. She remains quiet until they reach one of the roadside inns he favors on this journey, and when they're settled and fed and preparing to sleep, asks a question he does not expect: "May I see what it looks like?"

"What what looks like?"

Moira gestures to her chest and looks at his throat as her cheeks color. "When chaos heals."

Slowly, silently, Felix unlaces his shirt and pulls it over his head. He holds it against his torso as she brings her fingers to her lips, eyes widening. He keeps his voice low as he says, "Ysa cut me open." He drags a finger across the scarring, then spreads all five wide. "She cast into the tissue that was no longer needed and ordered it to break down. When it was finished, she shaped the skin and stitched me back together."

"Did it hurt?" Her fingertips are cool against his skin as she tentatively reaches for him.

"If I took a knife to you, would it hurt?"

Moira winces. "Point taken."

Felix feels like a young boy again, heart fluttering at the lightest touch. He relaxes his arm and bares the rest of his stomach, allowing her to imagine a life so different from her own. When she asks about specific wounds, he tells her about them: the burns, the knives, the bites. It's only when her fingers brush against his waistband that he clears his throat and steps back to tug his shirt on.

The next day, she is full of questions. Too full. Bursting at the seams with wonder.

"It's different for everyone," he snips when she asks *again* about how other mages align their intention with their magic. "Some don't think, just cast on instinct. Some don't. I imagine you might like it slow. I do."

"Can you do it quickly?"

"Yes, but it wipes me out." It is only when she snickers that he flushes crimson, and he doesn't allow her to get a word in before he urges Dirk into a gallop to put some distance between them.

They're days out from Baneston when the forest erupts around them. One second, Felix is teasing Moira about the scarf she's managed to lose just days after purchasing it; the next, he's laid out under several dreaders, one of which appears to have been a man once. Moira is screaming something, but Felix's focus is on the wolf's jaws tearing into his shoulder. As he cries out, he acts on instinct.

Magic pours into the wolf's body when Felix slaps a hand onto its snarling face, and he howls along with the creature as he takes it apart from the inside: unhooking tendon from bone, bursting arteries, rending muscle, fusing vertebrae. Anything he can think of, as fast as he can think of it, before he moves onto the remaining two. And then, when they're all little more than sacks of mince stewing in their own fluids, he hurls himself blindly at the sound of Moira's voice.

There is a dreader, and there is Moira beneath it, and there is so much blood between them.

He cannot say it is easy to dispatch the creature. He cannot say it's hard. All he can say, through lips coated in reeking viscera, is, "Where did they hurt you?"

"The horses," she wheezes.

"*Moira.*" Felix reaches for her, but halts when she shoves herself further back through the mud. Her face is porcelain pale, her whole body trembling as she stares at him with mounting horror. "Moira, I—"

"Our *supplies,* fool," she says. Or, attempts to say—it all comes out choked and wretched. "They—I think—Just . . . *go.*"

And so he does.

The animals bolted with several no-longer-human dreaders on their tails, and Felix spares himself a brief second of sadness for Daisy, who lays gutted, food for the dreader Felix dispatches with great prejudice. Before he's finished, he hears Dirk's panicked whinny from around the bend in the road, and he doesn't make it more than a few steps before the sound cuts off with a gurgling wheeze.

Felix curses.

He does what he has to do.

Dreaders always die easier than men. Felix stands above the pile of corpses and stares sightlessly down, hands trembling as his magic dissipates. When there's nothing left to stain his skin but the blood he's spilt, his knees hit the ground and he cannot stop himself from defiling Dirk's torn neck with the meager contents of his stomach. Already, the telltale sear of a migraine is lighting his head up from the inside. He is not built for this, the offensive quick-on-your-feet casting that some mages prefer. Allowing his magic to boil through him and overtake his senses has always left him reeling.

He wipes his mouth with the back of his hand and regrets it when randic blood bursts upon his tongue. Stumbling to his feet, he takes several wobbly steps before vomiting again. Dirk's glassy eye stares up at him as though even in death, he's disappointed in the pathetic show Felix is putting on.

He is faring no better by the time he makes it back to Moira, who regards him warily. "You were bleeding," he slurs. "Le—Lemme s-see. I can stopp't."

"Keep your hands away from me." Her voice is thin, but the horror comes through clear as day. "You're filthy."

Felix flinches. "Horses're dead."

"Was it your doing?"

"What? Why?"

Moira takes several steps back as Felix fumbles for one of the trees on the side of the road, and she does not seem inclined to answer the simple questions his muzzy head is already having a hard time latching onto. "You didn't tell me you cast like *that.* Who taught you? It's monstrous. You're . . ."

"Ysa," he says, like that'll appease her.

"The healer."

Felix needs to sit down. He does so without ceremony, only a breathy whine that crawls out of him when his ruined shoulder—already knitting itself together under what's left of his shirt—drags against the bark. "Please," he says. Please, *what,* he can't say, but he shuts his eyes and hugs himself to stop his traitorous hands from reaching for her. It has been years since the last time he did something as stupid as this—and then, it was one man, not a small horde of dreaders.

He inhales through his nose and attempts not to be sick again.

"Did you kill the thrice-damned horses, Felix?" Moira presses. Shoves, more like, as though more force behind the words will separate the truth from the lies she seems to suspect he's spelling. *"Answer."*

"No!"

He can hear her boots scuffing the dirt, but she doesn't approach. She says, "I will take care of it."

Felix can't help himself—when she begins to walk away, he pleads for her and scoots across the dirt like a dog on a rug. The raging headache has him crushed in its grip now, and the effort makes his blurry vision vignette. "I protected," he mumbles. "I'm good. I'm *good.*"

"You undid them entirely!" Moira's face is a rictus of disgust, all deep wrinkles and twisted rage, and he feels the force of it like a fist to the gut. "You *unmade* them."

"Yes." He doesn't have the energy to argue.

"They were *people* once."

"Mm."

"And you—You just."

"Moira." Felix's guts are in his throat again. "The point."

"You're . . ." She trails off and takes one tentative step toward him. He lifts his wobbly head to watch her disgust give way to horrified worry. "Oh, Felix, your throat, it's—The dreader must've—"

"'M fine," he says, slapping a hand over the wound and regretting it immediately.

"You're not."

And Felix does not argue, because the ground is making an unkind acquaintance with his face, and he does not have it in him to fight off the darkness any longer.

Waking is similarly unkind. Golden light assaults him through his closed eyelids, and the chill of early spring has sunk its teeth deep into his aching body. He hears a soft whicker nearby. When he attempts to sit up, cool hands push him back onto a bedroll he did not spread for himself. "Whossere," he mumbles.

"You're all right," is his awed non-answer. "Felix, you're *fine*."

He groans.

"Well, not quite, but you're not dead," Moira says, much closer, and Felix opens his eyes to the sight of her face hovering inches above his. He blinks owlishly before she says, "Hello."

"You stayed."

"And you scared me near to death, so yes, it's a surprise to us both." Moira slides a careful hand below Felix's shoulders and assists him as he pushes up on his elbows to get a look around. It's evening. He isn't sure whether it's tomorrow's evening or today's. He supposes it doesn't matter. The soft thud of hooves against dirt forces his head to the side, but Moira doesn't allow him to look too far before she's forcing his gaze back to hers, rambling the entire time.

"I've never seen anyone cast like that in my life. *Never* do that again. It's disgusting. And your wounds! Hells, you should be dead several times over, but they're just gone. Like it never happened! What did you *do?*"

"Water," Felix croaks.

"Here."

When he's drained half the waterskin, too slow to be doing anything but dawdling and too quick to make sense of everything racing through his head, he pushes Moira away and pats himself down with shaky hands. He twists around to see Dirk coming up behind him, intent on nibbling his hair, and he doesn't think the sudden lump in his throat is new scar tissue from the wolf's jaws. The blood and sick has all been washed away; still, he feels vile, as though his skin is raw from overexposure to the forge fire. When he sees Daisy grazing to his left, he snaps, "What did *you* do?"

"Cleaned you."

"The horses?" He feels panic seeping into his voice and can do nothing to stop it. "They were torn apart—did you . . . How? Resurrection is *vile.*"

She huffs, but there's very little heat in it. She does not attempt to justify herself. Mostly, she just looks tired. Beaten. Her shoulders slump as she sits back on her heels, and she frowns as she stares at her hands folded in her lap. She does not mince her words.

"I watched your torn throat knit itself together without any intervention. That doesn't just happen. And the rest of your wounds too; they're just . . . gone.

"I felt something," she continues, "when I was setting you back to rights. There's something in you that craves the touch of my magic. Or even just the touch of creation."

"So I'm a freak. An aberration. What of it?"

Moira flinches. "I didn't say that."

"Spit it out, Moira."

"I think you might have been there," she whispers, unable to look at him, "when the Sundering happened. Kestra's child was never fou—"

"No." Felix's denial is swift and decisive, as is his departure from the conversation. He hears Moira crashing through the underbrush behind him as he stalks through the forest, blazing a path toward anywhere that doesn't involve this line of discussion. Branches tear at his face and clothes, but he pays them no heed, using their clatter to drown out her insistence at closing the gaping wound he's ignored with varying degrees of success for the better part of a decade and a half.

"Feli—" she begins, wrapping her fingers around his wrist.

"Don't *touch* me," he spits, yanking his arm away as he spins to face her, venom on his tongue.

"I'm my da's son, all right? A smith's boy. That's all I've ever been. It's all I *want* to be. Maybe it's different for you, locked away in your ivory towers, but people like me don't *get* to be more than what we were made to be. *Mother?*" Felix barks an incredulous laugh. "Do you know how hard I've fought to forget the fact I don't have one? Do you know how many times I've cursed a faceless shade for having the *audacity* to bring me into this world? She left me to die, Moira, and I can't even do that properly.

"They call Kestra a god, you know, in Baneston. And I have never, *ever* wanted to walk in a god's footsteps. I am not Kestra's son. I won't be."

Moira swallows hard. "There are people who suspect she birthed a daughter."

"Good for them. Let the daughter rot."

"Felix." Moira looks stricken.

"This conversation is over," he says. "I'll ride with you to Baneston, because I promised that much. After that, you're on your own."

"Felix."

"Go." He bares his teeth in a snarl. "Be your own fucking hero. I won't do it."

Moira walks away from him with tears rolling down her cheeks and a hand clapped over her mouth. Some distant part of him—the man who is not the panicked boy frantically trying to stuff the ghost of girlhood into the pit of Felix's past—knows he should feel guilty about this. Everything else feels raw, like a wound spread open for Ysa's inspection.

He is many things.

He cannot be the child of the woman who helped sunder the north.

Still, he can do nothing to stop the way that that particular shard of information aligns itself with what he has never wanted to acknowledge.

While the first leg of their journey was quiet, the ride to Baneston is *silent*. Felix does his best to enjoy the gentle sway of Dirk's back below him, to enjoy the fond nibbling and the eagerness in his steps when Felix gives him free rein, but all he can think of are the wide swaths of skin where Dirk's coat hasn't yet regrown. He thinks of Moira, alone, attempting to focus her power to knit the horses' broken bodies together. He thinks of Moira, alone, watching his own body perform miracles he's long since tired of.

He thinks of Moira, and he feels sick.

Baneston appears first as a dark spot against the base of the Spine, surrounding both sides of the mountain pass before fading away to field and forest around its edges. Felix can point out individual farmsteads even from a distance—he's run through them all at one point or another, and caught the back of several hands for indulging himself with fresh fruit from their orchards or vegetables from garden plots. Past the fields lies the city proper: a sprawling mess of wood and stone, its buildings stuck haphazardly together like they're nothing more than a giant's discarded playthings. Birds wheel around the town center, where he suspects someone—perhaps multiple someones—swing from the gallows. (When he was young, the corpses scared him. Now, the thought of them is almost a comfort—no matter how far he wanders, it's good to know the City of Swords still rules with a blade in one hand and a rope in the other.)

Moira wilts in her saddle as they draw closer. Already, raucous laughter spills out of open taverns on the outskirts, as do the drunks it originates from. One of them pitches toward Daisy's flank, and Felix does not hesitate to drive his boot into the man's shoulder to shove him back into his friend. They both tumble into the mud. When they begin to protest, Felix silences them with a stony stare.

"Ain't that Tobin's boy?" one asks.

Belligerently, the other bellows, "Hey! Tobin's boy! Get back here!"

He offers them no response, nor does he acknowledge Moira's wide-eyed stare as they weave the horses through the increasing press of people. Though they're several streets away from the main square, vendors' cries filter through the air along with the reek of smoke, unwashed bodies, and best-unnamed alley muck. He carefully skirts Tobin's forge, choosing instead to pick his way through the debris that litters the dirt cart path behind this row of houses and shops.

Ysa's apothecary is obvious even from the back. Her thatched roof is the neatest of any nearby, and the small yard between the house and her small barn is meticulously organized. Felix hitches their horses and leads Moira to the back door, just raising his knuckles to rap on it when it flies open.

"Felix Grey," says Ysa Andira, still an imposing figure despite the way the years have worn on her. "Is it *ever* good to see you." She reaches up to cup his cheeks and draws their foreheads together, and Felix can't help the fond smile that cracks him from ear to ear.

"Hello, baba."

Her grip turns clinical, and he suffers her inspection with all the dignity he is afforded, which is very little indeed. "Hells, boy, you look like you've been through it. Did you take your friend on the adventure, too?" She lets him go with a flick to the forehead, and he grimaces as he rubs the spot. "I thought I taught you to play nice with others."

"He's been nice enough," Moira tells the ground.

"What's your name, girl?"

"Mo—"

"Ysa," Felix interrupts, cutting Moira off with a curt gesture. "Mind if we come in?"

She catches his urgency. "Give me ten minutes to shoo out the customers and close up. I'll be with you in a bit."

Those ten minutes are the longest of Felix's life. He stares at everything but Moira, fixing his attention on the crows overhead. He has to squint hard against the sun. Moira, who stopped attempting to bridge the newfound distance between them on the second day in the saddle, sits on a haybale next to the chicken coop and attempts to lure any one of the clucking hens nearer. When Ysa returns, it's with an offer of a basin to wipe the road from their face and hands, and then an offer of tea. It isn't until they're several minutes past introductions and into trite pleasantries that she turns to Felix with the look that invites—orders—him to explain himself.

"She wants to fix the Sundering," he states.

Ysa does not laugh. Instead, she looks at Moira, looks back to Felix, and sets her cup on the saucer with a definitive *click.* "She's got power in her."

"Krynn was my father."

The statement earns her a hiss of disapproval before Ysa asks Felix, "Where'd you pick this one up?"

He sighs. "Reiva's place."

"I tracked him down," Moira admits, like it wasn't Felix who laid in wait.

Ysa sucks on her teeth for several seconds, allowing the silence to sprout legs and begin to wander before she tells Moira, "Best be cautious with that kind of talk 'round here, sweetheart. Plenty of folks're liable to gut you for mentioning that name. Me, now . . . well." She chuckles. It does nothing to break the tension that's fallen across the table. "My boy seems to trust you, and it don't take much to convince me the sundering requires attention, but a pretty Aethran sniffing around about mages'll raise more'n a few hackles. Plenty of us remember your father—they'll not look kindly on you."

"I see."

"Do you have a bed free?" Felix asks, tipping his head toward Moira. "She'll need one before she heads north."

"Before *she* heads north, Felix?"

He stares at the ripple in the tea caused by his trembling hand before setting it down, pushing back his chair and saying, "I need to go. Need to talk to da."

Ysa calls after him as he all but flies out the back door, unable to shake the shame that clings to him like dog shit to boots. He is filled with trepidation; still, he cannot stop himself from bypassing Dirk and running up the back lane to the familiar door of home. When he bursts in, chest heaving, his father barely glances up from the ledger he's got spread out across the back table.

"You in trouble, Fe?"

"Did you ever suspect Kestra might have been my mother?"

That gives Tobin pause. He closes the book and looks over the top of his glasses at Felix. "You ever heard of sayin' hello first?"

"Hello, da. Did you e—"

Tobin waves the rest of the question away with the well-wrought steel arm attached to his left shoulder. "Sit." When Felix does, he says, "Yes."

"That's it?"

"Does it need explanation? Simple enough statement to me." Tobin sighs and props his chin in his right hand, his ruined face twisting in a rueful smile. His deep-set eyes rove over Felix, drinking him in after nearly two years of time away. "You look tired."

"Things on my mind."

"Someone's been telling you tales."

"Yeah. The only other mage I've found who comes close to matching me in power." Felix pulls out his usual chair and turns it, sitting with his arms folded across the back and his face planted firmly in the space between them. "Someone who thinks Krynn himself fucked her mother."

"And . . . is this someone . . . correct?"

"Yes. Maybe. I don't know. I think—" Felix takes a deep breath, and doesn't stop speaking. He has never been able to hide from his da: not the good, not the bad, not the ugly. It's something in the way Tobin leans in and fixes his eyes on a speaker. He listens with every part of himself.

Felix tells him the facts about his month with Moira. He lists them with the same precision he'd use to report a contract's fulfillment, but he winces at the way he comes out callous. Part of him marvels at the miracle that is the lack of Ysa's appearance to scold him about whatever Moira's surely telling her while Felix spills his guts. And then, through clenched teeth, he tells Tobin of Moira's plans to heal the Sundering, and her suspicions as to why he might be the second key element in said plan.

"I remember bits and pieces of my time beyond the Spine," he finally says. "No child would have survived that. None could, not without magical intervention. And chaos is not known for keeping even its adult mages alive. If I was there, even barely alive, then Krynn's magic might've . . . helped."

Tobin regards him for several long moments, but says nothing.

"Were you ever going to tell me?" Felix mumbles.

With a grunt of effort, Tobin stands and pulls Felix up into a crushing embrace. Felix feels his da's chest expand with a mighty breath, and he sighs along with him. "What mattered to us was that you were all right. That's what we wanted for you."

"Oh," Felix says, voice small.

"Felix," Tobin says, pulling back to grip Felix's shoulder. "You were—are—*my* son. You are loved, you fool. That is a fact of life." He shakes his head. "I was always going to love you, regardless of who bore you. But this Moira girl, now—can't imagine she had that, growing up a mage at court."

"I hurt her," Felix whispers. "I didn't mean to, but she just . . . She pushed me." Felix looks up with bleary eyes. "I left her with Ysa. I didn't trust anyone else to keep her safe."

"You care for this woman," Tobin says, and Felix watches as the pieces of the puzzle fall into alignment. "You do!"

"Against my better judgement." When Tobin cuffs him lightly upside the head, he hisses and amends, "Yes, hells."

Tobin lets Felix go and sits back down with a heavy huff, eyes turned toward the ceiling in silent supplication. "Why I thought raisin' a boy might be easier," he laments. "Ysa's going to have *both* our hides if you don't make this right, lad. You'll be apologizing."

"Yes, da."

"And you'll be doing the right thing, won't you." Tobin raises one bushy eyebrow, but Felix does not need the prompting to stand, make his exit, and go to do what he knows he must.

ΦΦΦ

Once upon a not-so-distant future, across the not-so-distant peaks of the Spine that splits Avetri, there will stand an army. At its head will stand a man and a woman, hand in hand and bathed in dawn's golden light. They will kneel, and they will place their palms against the earth, and they will begin to toil. They will toil, and their army will toil, and they will not stop until the land is once again hale.

They will lead.

They will love.

And finally, after their long years of duty, they will *live*.

ABOUT THE AUTHOR

A.C. BAUER is your average author caricature. When he's not writing, he's complaining about writing. When he's writing, he's complaining even harder.

Summoning him is as easy as leaving a cup of coffee unattended (or saying, "Pspsps, I've written a fresh new white-haired trauma twink for you.").

He developed a passion for fantasy in early childhood, concerning librarians and classmates alike with the number of books he devoured in any given week. Ever since, he's endeavored to channel that passion (and his queer experience) through his own creative work.